To Debi, Mark, Addie, and Stephanie:
Dearest family, I hope you always
feel your best. God bless!
– KW

To Noah and Levi,
who once made me feel sick,
but now only ever make me feel better.
–JC

SIMON AND SCHUSTER
First published in Great Britain in 2007 by Simon & Schuster UK Ltd
1st Floor, 222 Gray's Inn Road, London, WC1X 8HB
A CBS COMPANY
This paperback edition published in 2007

Originally published in 2007 by Margaret K. McElderry Books,
an imprint of Simon & Schuster Children's Publishing Division, New York

The text for this book is set in Adobe Caslon.
The illustrations are rendered in acrylic paint.

A CIP catalogue record for this book is available from the British Library upon request.

ISBN: 978 1 84738 066 1

Printed in China

3 5 7 9 10 8 6 4 2

Bear Feels Ill

Karma Wilson

illustrations by Jane Chapman

SIMON AND SCHUSTER

London   New York   Toronto   Sydney

Alone in his cave
as the autumn wind blows,
Bear feels achy
with a stuffed-up nose.

He tosses and he turns,
all huddled in a heap.
Bear feels tired,
but he just can't sleep.

He sniffs and he sneezes.
He whiffs and he wheezes.
And the bear
                    feels
                              ill.

His friends gather round.
"Come out, Bear, and play."
Bear shakes his head.
"I'm too poorly today."

Mouse mutters, "Oh my,
Bear's head is too hot."
Hare says, "We will help!
Here's a warm, cosy spot."

Bear mumbles and he moans. He grumbles and he groans.

And the bear
feels
ill.

Mouse squeezes Bear tight.
He whispers in his ear,
"It'll be just fine.
Your friends are all here."

Badger fetches water.
Gopher cooks the broth
while Mole soothes Bear
with a cool, wet cloth.

They cover Bear up and he drinks from a cup.

But he still feels ill.

Raven says, "*Caw!*
Come along, Owl and Wren.
Let us go gather herbs
to bring back to the den."

They coax Bear to sip
just a smidgen of tea.
"You'll feel better soon,"
says Mouse. "Wait and see."

Bear shakes and he shivers. He coughs and he quivers.

And he still

feels

ill.

The friends fuss and fret.
The friends cook and care.
They keep a close eye
on their poor ill Bear.

They all talk in whispers.
They walk on tippy toes.
They sing lullabies.
Then the bear starts to doze.

They watch Bear for hours.
"We've done all we could."

Then the bear wakes up.

And the bear
feels
GOOD!

Bear cries, "I'm all better.
I'm feeling like new.
I'm not hot and achy.
It's all thanks to you!

"Let's celebrate now.
Let's go out and play.
Let's jump in the leaves.
Let's frolic all day!"

Then Mouse starts to wheeze and Hare starts to sneeze . . .

and the friends feel ill!

Bear murmurs, "Don't worry,"
and tucks them in bed.
He bundles them up
and he kisses each head.

He tells all his friends,
"You'll soon feel like new.
You took care of me . . .
now I'll take care of you."